THE

BIRTHDAY

Story and pictures by

Val Biro

"Tomorrow is Blob's birthday.
Let's make him a birthday cake,"
said Gobbler.

The monsters made a beautiful cake,
with candles on top. They put it on
the table.

Then they went to buy Blob some
monster birthday presents.

Gobbler bought a Monster Snakes and
Ladders set, with real snakes.

5

Warty bought a Monster Gorilla Mask,
and Fuzzy bought a Monster T. Rex
that went ROAR.

They put the presents round the table.
But the cake had disappeared!
"Who took the cake?" they cried.

"I did!" said the giant monster from next door.
"And very nice it was, too!"